### Put Beginning Readers on the Right Track with
### ALL ABOARD READING™

The All Aboard Reading series is especially for beginning readers. Written by noted authors and illustrated in full color, these are books that children really and truly *want* to read—books to excite their imagination, tickle their funny bone, expand their interests, and support their feelings. With four different reading levels, All Aboard Reading lets you choose which books are most appropriate for your children and their growing abilities.

**Picture Readers—for Ages 3 to 5**
Picture Readers have super-simple texts with many nouns appearing as rebus pictures. At the end of each book are 24 flash cards—on one side is the rebus picture; on the other side is the written-out word.

**Level 1—for Preschool through First Grade Children**
Level 1 books have very few lines per page, very large type, easy words, lots of repetition, and pictures with visual "cues" to help children figure out the words on the page.

**Level 2—for First Grade to Third Grade Children**
Level 2 books are printed in slightly smaller type than Level 1 books. The stories are more complex, but there is still lots of repetition in the text and many pictures. The sentences are quite simple and are broken up into short lines to make reading easier.

**Level 3—for Second Grade through Third Grade Children**
Level 3 books have considerably longer texts, use harder words and more complicated sentences.

All Aboard for happy reading!

For Nolan—J.D.

For Steve—M.S.

Special thanks to Amie Gallagher, Assistant Producer, American Museum of Natural History, Hayden Planetarium.

*Library of Congress Cataloging-in-Publication Data*

Dussling, Jennifer.
    Stars / by Jennifer Dussling ; illustrated by Mavis Smith.
      p.    cm. — (All aboard reading)
    Summary: Explains what stars are and what people have thought about them in different times and places.
    1. Stars—Juvenile literature. [1. Stars.] I. Smith, Mavis, ill.
II. Title. III. Series.
QB801.7.D87  1996
523.8—dc20
                                            95-24763
                                                 CIP

ISBN 0-448-41149-0 (GB)  A B C D E F G H I J          AC

ISBN 0-448-41148-2 (pbk)  A B C D E F G H I J

ALL
ABOARD
READING™
Level 1
Preschool-Grade 1

# STARS

By Jennifer Dussling
Illustrated by Mavis Smith

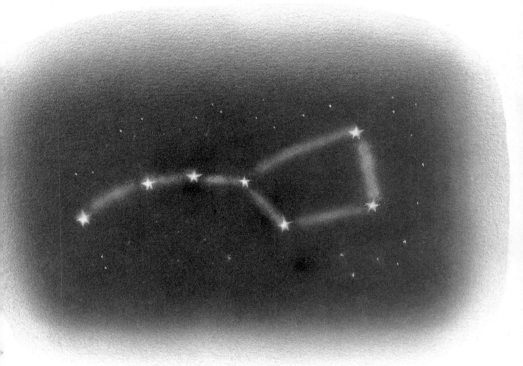

Grosset & Dunlap • New York

Look at the night sky.
What do you see?
Lots and lots
of white dots.
Stars!

Long ago
some people said
the sky was like a bowl
turned upside down.
It sat on the tops
of mountains.

The stars were holes—
holes poked in the bowl.

Some people
made up stories
about the stars.

One group of stars
looked like a crown.
People said it was
the crown of a princess.
A god loved the princess.
But then she died.

The god put her crown
in the sky—
so he could see it forever.

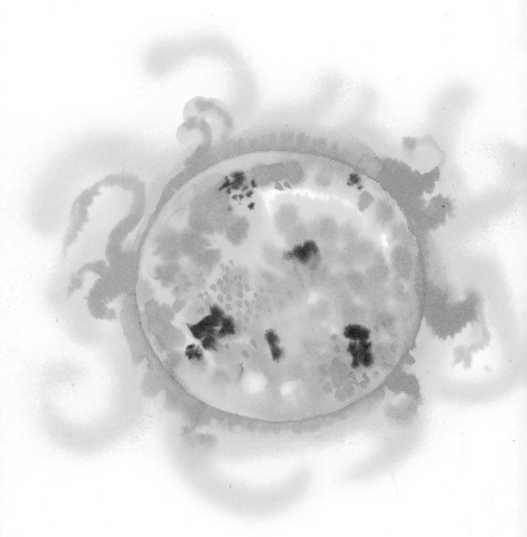

Today we know
what a star really is.
A star is a ball of burning gas.
It is very hot and very bright.

Stars come in different colors.
There are yellow stars
and blue stars.
There are red stars
and orange stars too.

But when you look up
at the sky,
most stars look white.

Star

Earth

Stars are big—
very, very big.
They only look small
because they are
so far away.

Think of the biggest star
and Earth like this.
You have a soccer ball
in one hand.
That is the big star!
You have one little
grain of sand in your
other hand.
That is Earth.

One star is closer
than the rest.
It is not the biggest star.
But it looks big
because it is so near.
We feel its heat.
This star is the sun.

Without the sun,
no plants could grow.
In the day
the sun is so bright
we cannot see other stars.
But they are there
just the same.

Can you ever
see stars in the day?
Yes!

Sometimes the moon
blocks out the light
from the sun.
This is called an eclipse.
(You say it like this: ee-clips.)

There are special ways
to look at an eclipse
without hurting your eyes.

During an eclipse,

the day gets darker and colder.

The stars come out.

And some animals go to sleep.

They think it is night.

But in a few minutes,

the moon moves.

The sun comes back out.

It's day again!

Long ago
sailors used the stars
to help them cross the ocean.

They made
a map of the stars.
It showed them
where they were going.

Stars still help people
find their way.
One group of seven stars
shows which way is north.

These stars look like
different things
to different people.

A bear and three birds.

A hook.

A wagon.

29

We say it is a big soup spoon.

We call it the Big Dipper.

Look up!

Can you find the Big Dipper?

It's there in the night sky
with all the other millions
and millions of stars.